TAMMY GEARY

BECOME WANTED ENTERTAINMENT
PRESENTS

ART STORY
ONE

Created and Composed by
DAVID STERLING GEARY

All rights reserved. No part of this book may be reproduced in any manner without written permission except in the case of brief quotations included in critical articles and reviews. For information, please contact the author.

Copyright © 2024 by
BECOME WANTED ENTERTAINMENT

Printed and Bound in the United States of America

All characters appearing in this work are fictitious.
Any resemblance to real persons, living or dead, is purely coincidental.

ISBN: 979-8-218-49843-6

Original cover art contributed by: David Sterling Geary
All artwork including photography, cover art, and the East Freeland logo Copyright © 2024 by
BECOME WANTED ENTERTAINMENT

BECOME WANTED ENTERTAINMENT
First Printing
www.becomewanted.com

CHAMPIONING DIVERSITY

EAST FREELAND: ART STORY ONE

You can't escape the cinematic vibe expressed through this Korean-American author's imagination, where Eastern martial arts coexist with raw police power and traces of Western legends, creating a fierce experience that packs a real punch with a remarkable cultural spin.

Born from his many things of various sorts, you can sense the diverse threads of David's narrative as they come together to form a portrayal that plunges deeper than surface-level fun and speaks directly to your heart.

So, immerse yourself in this masterfully drafted fiction and turn the page where you'll find that family becomes a haven, courage becomes a battle cry, justice becomes a beacon of hope, and forgiveness becomes the breakthrough that sets us free.

PREFACE

EAST FREELAND: ART STORY ONE

As the sun began its ascent, its emerging rays exposed the unforgiving slums of a shady town well hidden in the great metropolis of Freeland City. Pitched lamps along a particular avenue dimly lit the tattered pavement and battered trash cans that lined its sidewalks, introducing a community shunned and nearly forgotten.

Loose litter, taken by the day's breeze, tumbled near various storefronts, all safeguarded behind steel gates until opening hours. In this poverty-stricken area, those who valued their businesses and the opportunities they produced were best to protect them.

Among the assorted chain of customary retail marts, Whispering Blossoms was an example of magnificence and evenness that stood as evidence of the neighborhood's enduring grace; the store was a wonderful thing. Its brick exterior exuded refinement and resilience, mirroring the blooming flowers it sheltered while the shop's expansive windows

PREFACE

were carefully garnished to display the store's stunning floral arrangements, appropriate for the many customers Whispering Blossoms has welcomed for several years.

He was just a little man. Minutes before opening, the venerable florist could often be found amidst the fragrant blooms, donning his traditional blue hanbok.

His face, etched with a roadmap of wisdom, was a testament to the passage of time by each line, and yet, his hands still moved with practiced grace, tending to each orchid as if it held a cherished memory with a deep love for the brilliant world of flowers he had devoted his life to.

Passed down through generations, Mr. Ko's trade, by small steps, became a romance about a family's promise, and amidst the rich bouquets for sale, customers were also drawn to the owner's delicate spirit and the wealth of understanding he willingly shared.

Then, as the calm atmosphere of the shop

EAST FREELAND: ART STORY ONE

reached its peak, it was shattered by the intrusion of motor oil, machine exhaust, and three elusive bikers clad in helmets, hoodies, jeans, and worn-out high-top sneakers.

SMASH!

"Mr. Ko!" The intruders bore unmistakable signs of the rebellious lifestyle as their motorcycles parked outside were embellished with Hangul displayed along their black bikes, similar to those inscribed on their hoodies and helmets. "You have been doing business on our turf for a very long time." In this town, street racers were known for their aggressive presence; therefore, a combination of speed, mastery, and fashion was ideal for their involvement in the city's prohibited racing society.

"What is it that you want from me?" he asked.

"We want our cut on all of your transactions for doing business on *18th Street*."

"I don't have that kind of money."

PREFACE

"Yeah?" Then, with a subtle gesture, two bikers began flipping Mr. Ko's shop upside down, smashing chairs, ripping flowers from their pots, and turning tables.

"Oh, no...please stop?" The invasion sent shockwaves through Mr. Ko's heart. His eyes widened with worry just as the trust he had earned from the community was suddenly under threat, and he couldn't bear to see his haven of blossoms further tarnished. "Please, I'll pay, I'll pay!" he pleaded. The florist was washed with fear as he helplessly faced the shattered entrance and broken glass shards of lost hope scattered across the floor.

"Damn right you'll pay...tag this joint!"

Reveling in their sadistic display of power and control, they finally revealed spray paint cans and, with aimed arrogance, commenced defacing the remaining walls of Whispering Blossoms with their gang's notorious insignia—*7 Streeters*. Each stroke of humiliation felt like a dagger twisting in Mr. Ko's heart

EAST FREELAND: ART STORY ONE

as he watched on helplessly. But when despair threatened to consume him, a watchful character emerged, leaning against a mighty red Z6-R.

"Enough already."

"Ricky," whispered Mr. Ko.

Decked out in a worn brown leather jacket, black pants, snazzy sunglasses, and durable hand gloves that showcased his readiness for combat, his commanding voice cut through the tension like a switchblade while he lit a cigarette perched on his lips. The car's engine rumbled with a low, menacing tone, mirroring a man bent on removing the crew who threatened Mr. Ko.

"More are coming!" spoke the bravest of the 7 Streeters.

"Let them," Ricky replied.

Thus, as the distant roar of incoming motorcycles grew louder, the bold owner of the Z6-R steeled himself for the forthcoming battle in anticipation.

PREFACE

Up to then, Mr. Ko sought safety by a nearby counter as he, too, braced himself for a showdown that would prove to be like no other.

Surrounded by not three but now eleven 7 Streeters, Ricky pocketed his police badge, flicked his still-burning cigarette, and readied his fists.

"You think you can take on all of us?" they taunted, eager to test their mettle against him.

"Absolutely," he answered. "You've disrespected Mr. Ko and have committed an injustice under my jurisdiction, and as long as I'm enlisted with Unity East, your hold on this town will continue to crumble!"

Ricky's fierce proclamation struck fear into each 7 Streeter standing before him, and although a street fight had just begun, a malevolent tempest was looming on the horizon.

ECHOES OF HAN

ECHOES OF HAN

East Freeland, where heritage, ambition, and individuality were ever connected and where every face told a beautiful story, drummed with the spirit of Han. Unlike its neighboring divisions in Freeland City, it was a place to remember for its enchantment and distinctiveness.

Here, the echoes of age-old teachings resonated with the people as they graced the footpaths with a passion for fashion and a playful splash of color that symbolized tradition, jubilation, and, of course, good fortune.

Small businesses were trimmed with legendary motifs that embodied the balance between history and progress upon which the town thrived. A strong sense of culture mixed with the yarns of community formed an unbreakable bond that survived through generations.

Among honorable martial arts schools scattered throughout the inner city, the Hwarang Spirit Dojang opened its doors to those

EAST FREELAND: ART STORY ONE

seeking discipline and enlightenment. Instructors at this school led by example, for they were responsible for passing down the ancient lore of martial arts to their bravest students so that they could carry on their teachings for generations to come.

Dignified academic institutions like the Jeongseon Wisdom Archive dotted the district, offering their boundless shelves filled with tales of mystery, note-worthy narratives, and intensely sought-after understanding to the thinkers of the world of learning.

Amidst the art of fighting, East Freeland's notorious entertainment film studio, Soaring Pictures, stood as yet another driving force of creativity and collaboration, connecting directors, writers, and actors to bring their spellbinding masterpieces to life while simultaneously carving a lasting niche in the pantheon of cinematic history.

While these industries relished in their respective ownership, the heart of this spirit-

ECHOES OF HAN

ed community stood the city's noble law enforcement agency: Unity East, a true emblem of justice and order, commanding respect and admiration from all who passed by.

Discreet Hangul characters championed the team's values just above the entrance encircled by a gorgeous garden pathway that seemed to stretch out a welcoming hand, making the command's ultimate goal – to serve and protect – feel instantly tangible.

From literature to martial arts-inspired action films policed under the watch of the Unity East, East Freeland celebrated its heritage while embracing the inner city's ability to withstand force without equal.

But on the opposite side of the town, a forbidden building, recognized by its cracked and colorless shell, could be seen blocks away as it continued to crumble with the debris from a vanquished era. Its scars stood as evidence of how one man managed to turn a street gang into an organized syndicate force

EAST FREELAND: ART STORY ONE

that tormented the city's citizens until one man from Unity East stepped up to put a stop to their criminal reign and buried their operation, both literally and figuratively.

UNITY EAST

EAST FREELAND: ART STORY ONE

Speeding down Han's path, the red Z6-R's driving force was felt not only in its sound but also in its visual impact.

VROOM!

The showy speedster broke through the air like a fierce thunderclap, commanding the attention of several cadet trainees exiting the grand headquarters with its mechanical might. The car's outcry hammered through the surrounding streets, causing many more to turn with curiosity and wonder. Hence, its sleek lines, gleaming paint, and bold design contributed to the aura of confidence surrounding the stylish vehicle.

Then, as the high-powered machine glided to a sharp finish, whispers of speculation and admiration began to ripple through their ranks. But when its engine cut and its rumble quickly subsided, the onlookers stood in awe, imagining a life beyond the ordinary and, for some, a life they had yearned for.

As Ricky pulled on the glass doors of

UNITY EAST

Unity East, he stepped into a realm where harmony and collaboration converged. His gaze swept across the grand archway that adorned the entrance, its intricate patterns inspired by traditional artistry seamlessly intertwining with elements reminiscent of everyday law enforcement symbols. This fusion symbolized the significance of purpose, defining a place where cultures intertwined to uphold justice.

Subtle yet meaningful Hangul was discreetly integrated into the design, serving as gentle reminders of the department's Asian roots and the diverse needlework of authorities within.

Journeying through the lobby, Ricky was drawn to the emblem displayed proudly above the entrance, a symbolic representation of the department's commitment to collaboration and shared values. Its design harmoniously combined the diversity of two worlds, thus capturing the spirit that pulsated through the precinct.

EAST FREELAND: ART STORY ONE

As he stepped further into the building, Ricky felt the agency's energy envelop him. The interior, an extension of the exterior's design, whispered stories of bravery and devotion imagined through exquisite, dream-like illustrations that reflected the cultural heritage of traditional policing.

Organized within the department's assignment area, police cadets in blue and white uniforms occupied several desks in a symphony of accordance. Their dedication to justice was even evident in their focused discussions, further demonstrating the shared purpose that bound them all together.

Compared to other precincts in Freeland City, Unity East was unique in its approach, and where the culture was deeply ingrained in the department, its cadets were expected to adhere to certain traditions and maintain a strict code of conduct at all times.

In this hallowed space, Ricky knew he had found his calling. The journey that led

UNITY EAST

him here, shaped by his unwavering sense of justice, had brought him to the heart of the police space.

With each stride, he welcomed the station's ethos, prepared to add to the heritage of this distinctive division with dignity, uprightness, and profound reverence for the mutual principles that directed them collectively.

And so, as Ricky took his place among the heroes of Unity East, the precinct embraced him as one of its own, and together, united under one umbrella, they were willing to make a difference, one act of collaboration at a time.

Holding up in the police station's main hall, a central thoroughfare where cadets from various departments often crossed, a blindfolded police operative clad in an impeccable blue tailored suit couldn't help but overhear Ricky's encounter at the floral shop on 18th Street. Thus, he tip-toed over to receive the account firsthand.

EAST FREELAND: ART STORY ONE

"Is that so?" Detective Lee, a marveled Special Crimes Expert, as inscribed on his nameplate, possessed a professional appearance and a tenacious dedication honed during his term at Unity East. His commitment to his duty and ability to navigate some of East Freeland's most complex investigations made him a force to be reckoned with both on and off the job. "So, you defeated Jung's gang all by yourself?" he asked. Although his eyes were concealed behind a red blindfold, his remaining traits, otherwise complemented by a faint trace of facial hair, exuded a stormy yet sophisticated virtue. Moreover, his lack of sight was not overtaken by his meticulously long black hair, unlike that of Ricky's.

"You better believe it, Jack!"

"It's Jackie."

"Yeah, yeah." Sauntering into Investigations, Ricky stopped momentarily and puffed out his chest before declaring, "So, when I arrived, there were too many of them to count,

UNITY EAST

and so, I became the *Tornado of Justice*, for I am this station's finest!" Nodding in fascination, Jackie acknowledged the rowdy cadet and sought to offer a word of wisdom through a delicately inquisitive inflection.

"Quite the spectacle, Ricky. Your martial prowess is certainly noteworthy. But remember, true strength isn't only about individual might. This precinct flourishes on the foundation of teamwork, for we're one unit; am I right?" Beaming with pride, however, Ricky dismissed Jackie's remarks and proceeded to the remaining departments to convey his meaningless narrative filled with ego and Karate.

"Hey…just stick to your reports, and I'll handle the 7 Streeters."

"Of course, Ricky; every part has its role," remarked the blind police operative, and as he sensed Ricky's departure, Jackie merely grinned. Ricky's response neither pleased nor angered him. At most, he valued his commit-

EAST FREELAND: ART STORY ONE

ment to rid East Freeland of the 7 Streeters and anyone else who dared to challenge the strength of Unity East.

#

As dusk settled over Freeland City, a solitary figure materialized beneath a flickering streetlamp across from the station, casting a crawly glow on the man's skeletal form cloaked in a fine Chinese-inspired suit. But that wasn't the odd characteristic about him. Bandages enshrouded the stranger's head and hands, leaving only his wrathful eyes seeable, crusty nostrils exposed, and a crinkled cigarette perched along the edges of his split lips.

With his sights fixed on Unity East, the outsider took a long drag from his burning cancer stick and exhaled before he spoke.

"So, the pieces are finally in motion," he murmured as the smoke, fleeing through his teeth, curled around his bandaged face.

A PLUM BLOSSOM PROMISE

EAST FREELAND: ART STORY ONE

The tenacious clicking of an ink pen emanating from a secured office introduced a dedicated cadet deeply engrossed in a report at her desk.

Much like the others at Unity East, she, too, was determined to crackdown on the lawlessness that tested her town's resolve by seeking justice for the innocent citizens harmed by the violent acts of the 7 Streeters.

She was as taintless as the smart glasses perched on the bridge of her runty nose, lending a touch of sophistication to her overall visage while highlighting her most purest features alongside her unwavering dedication to her work. Adhering to the precinct's dress regulations, her uniform consisted of a sleeveless ivory top tucked into a deep blue skirt and topped with a sleek beret that concealed her neatly kept hair pulled back. On the surface, she appeared to be the station's harmless cadet, but beyond the outfit, she would prove to be much much more.

A PLUM BLOSSOM PROMISE

This space, where she conducted her investigations, was a rumination of her individuality, passions, and the distinctiveness of her physical challenge, thoughtfully tailored to facilitate her use of a wheelchair while also fostering an atmosphere that motivated and empowered her.

Her surroundings were elevated with images commemorating moments of triumph and camaraderie, acting as a heartwarming recollection of her most treasured connections. Moreover, these photographs, among others, were deliberately placed at an elevation that allowed her to view them from her wheeled companion.

She was set for duty under the brilliant lighting fixtures, positioned at the ceiling's extremities by design, that showcased her extensive workstation equipped with accessible drawers for minor items, a safe compartment for sensitive documents, and a polished Jutte finished with a red cord, forged from the

EAST FREELAND: ART STORY ONE

finest steel in Freeland City, to combat the Unwanted if they were to breach the precinct.

The fusion of her dedication down-the-line to Unity East and perspective, beyond comparsison, brought as an examiner with a physical disability made her an indispensable resource to the station. But then, when the soundlessness shrouding her began to bulge, her awareness suddenly peaked when she sensed the presence of—

"Ricky?"

With a graceful movement, she wheeled herself away from her desk and into the corridors where the worries she held for her idol often gnawed at her whenever he was away. She understood his dedication to the cause, but fighting crime the way he did would only put his life and others near him at risk.

Upon turning the corner, she noticed a rare cluster of Plum Blossoms cleverly arranged on a compact surface anchored in the middle of the precinct's entrance hall.

A PLUM BLOSSOM PROMISE

Their mild petals, newly bloomed in soft shades of pink and white, added a tinge of windless beauty to the otherwise utilitarian space while creating a moment of serenity amid the stark reality of their everyday police operations.

Realizing the significance of this gentle gesture, her heart fluttered, for it spoke volumes for the state East Freeland was currently in. It was a fresh start at new beginnings and how our fearless initiatives could promise a better tomorrow.

Eager to locate the individual responsible for the kind effort, she spun around until Unity East's bravest cadet entered her line of sight.

"Ricky!" Her voice was filled with adoration and concern as she wheeled closer to him. "You never cease to amaze me," she said aloud, "But please, promise me that you'll take care out there, and when are you going to toss those silly sunglasses away?"

EAST FREELAND: ART STORY ONE

Her liveliness amused Ricky enough to make him smile, but as his hidden gaze met hers, he sensed the underlying suspicion in her remarks.

"Ah, Jenni, you worry too much. Besides, I'm your father's favorite…did you forget?" he said, and then, with his fists equipped, he struck the air to demonstrate that his Karate was better than the others in the whole department.

"Ricky!" she jabbed.

"Alright, alright! I promise to be cautious and not rely only on my strength but on wisdom. How about that?"

"That's better." Instantly, her worries dissipated, replaced by a renewed conviction while remembering the importance of cherishing every moment they had together. But amid their playful exchange, one notion still remained. "Ricky?"

"What's up?"

"Where did you find these flowers?" she

A PLUM BLOSSOM PROMISE

asked. Yet, before the shade-wearing cadet could respond—

"RICKY!"

Disturbing the division halls, a booming voice commanded attention and immediate compliance with an unmistakable air of authority and urgency.

"Oh no, father's upset," she said.

"MY OFFICE, NOW!"

Jenni's focus shifted from Ricky to the imperative call of duty, for she feared the worse for her most favored brother, who often managed to evade her father's grasp, but perhaps not this time.

"Don't you worry, little sister...he's always upset," he teased.

Grasping the urgency in her father's voice, she released him from her embrace, not without honoring the delicate flower he had gifted her.

"Don't allow your pride to overtake you, Ricky!" Jenni exclaimed.

THE GENTLE GIANT

THE GENTLE GIANT

Ricky stood before a considerable man seated behind a vast desk whose expression was hardened with disappointment. His leader was clad in uncompromising excellence, for his command office was garnished with various awards, mementos, and reminders of his distinguished career. Among them, a bronze statue of him as the former Sumo Champion of East Freeland proudly stood on a shelf, representing a daring man's unwavering commitment to his craft and the discipline he had honed some time before.

Surrounding them were a collection of reference materials, case files, and crime charts, meticulously arranged to reflect the man's attention to detail and commitment to thoroughness. It was a stretch where the lead watchman strategized, always prepared to face the complexities of his role. Framed photographs of the former champion alongside ex-city officials placed along the walls showcased his close connections with influ-

EAST FREELAND: ART STORY ONE

ential masters in the Asian community as a testament to the trust and admiration he had earned over the years.

Amidst the professional decor, personal touches could be found throughout the office. A meticulously cared-for bonsai tree sat on a corner of the Champion's worktop, symbolizing the tranquility he sought in the chaos that plagued his town, and there, along the razor's edge, was a steel nameplate displaying "The Head Watchman:" *First Sergeant Kato.*

"That car of yours draws too much attention," speaking from a qualified position in the study, a well-informed voice warned Ricky, prompting him to remain on point, and with respect, he did so.

"10-4."

"Stop it, Ricky," said Kato.

"My apologies, sir," Ricky replied, quickly containing another loose word from slipping through his teeth. Carefully arranged along Kato's back wall, photographs featur-

THE GENTLE GIANT

ing the two captured the depth of their relationship. They depicted the bond between a mentor and his adopted son, showcasing their shared journey. In some photos, serious discussions were evident in their expressions, reflecting their dedication to the pursuit of justice. While in others, warm smiles radiated, revealing the familial love and support that had grown between them over time.

"I spoke with Mr. Ko," he began. He admired his boldest Guardian for his fighting potential, which was evident. Yet, Kato understood that Ricky required further guidance to channel his strengths and energy more orderly. "He informed me that you faced those 7 Streeters again. That's the third time this season," he added. Just hours ago, Kato learned that Ricky had bravely defended Mr. Ko against the attackers, showing a glimmer of fearlessness amidst his reckless behavior.

"I hate 7 Streeters," Ricky interjected, giving way to the very reason he was sum-

EAST FREELAND: ART STORY ONE

moned in the first place. Thus, Kato steeled himself for a conversation that, despite his immense strength, he knew Ricky lacked restraint, and it was his responsibility to steer him toward self-improvement.

"Mr. Ko, kind-hearted and forgiving, expressed his willingness to overlook the damages you had inadvertently caused during the incident. However, as the highest-ranking officer of Unity East, I must address your outlandish stunts and remind you of the consequences that could have ensued." He was a prideful man in his well-earned fifties with a bullish presence that reflected his transition from a professional sumo wrestler to the revered law enforcement officer he became.

His face carried a sense of wisdom and grit. Adorning his face was a burly mustache, adding a touch of rugged masculinity to his countenance. The bushy thing symbolized his strength and decisiveness, mirroring his tenacity during his sumo wrestling days, and

THE GENTLE GIANT

as for the hair on his head, it was styled in a manner reminiscent of an athlete, each strand reflecting his attention to detail and his structured approach to his work.

"They won't stop...not until Jung pays for his crimes."

"You are right, and while your bravery was commendable, it is important to acknowledge the reckless manner in which you handled the situation," he explained, "You possess an incredible fighting force, Ricky, but power without discipline is dangerous. Your actions could have escalated, drawing more 7 Streeters, resulting in more damage and even a fatality," he concluded. "It is not how I want my police cadets to respond to disturbances in the future."

Ricky's expression, hidden vaguely behind his sunglasses, shifted, following a mere flicker of realization that crossed his features. He hadn't grasped the effects of his actions and the potential harm he could have caused

EAST FREELAND: ART STORY ONE

to Mr. Ko, and this chipped at his spirit.

"I waited for them," he started. "I wanted to send *him* a message, and I didn't care who got in my way." Ricky's gaze dropped, defeated by remorse. He recognized the gravity of his behavior and the need to explore another approach to what he considered harsh policing.

Kato permitted a moment for Ricky's admission to sink in. He deeply considered Ricky, yet he desperately needed him to understand the weight of his words.

"As the strongest cadet within this department, it is crucial that you start exercising restraint. We'll get him, but until then, your physical prowess must be matched by discernment and sound judgment, am I clear?" he emphasized.

"Yes, First Sergeant."

"Ricky, I want to share something with you. Is that alright?" he asked. His tone softened as their chat took an unexpected turn.

THE GENTLE GIANT

"Absolutely, sir." Though Kato's physical appearance may have been imposing, his inner character and unwavering dedication to his daughter, Jenni, truly defined him.

"I remember when Jenni was on the beat. I didn't think she could handle the pressure of being in uniform, but I was wrong." A faint smile crossed his lips as he imagined her accomplishments, now memories of the past. "She always approached her duties with thoughtfulness and exactness. My daughter understood that true strength was not only found in our physical capacities and our ability to make sound decisions, exercise self-control, and treat every individual with respect." His love for Jenni was transparent in how he supported her aspirations without her presence and despite her physical limitations. Kato's imperishable devotion added a layer of depth to his formidable presence, showcasing the complexity of his character overall. "Even after all that she had endured, she remained an influential addition to this department, which is why I expect more from you; do you understand?"

Ricky paused. He also recalled Jenni's past success and the tragedy that would forever haunt him and his First Sergeant.

"Yes, I understand." He was as still as the trees and brittle leaves in the fall, urging to be released.

"Good." Suddenly, his eyes grew thin, emphasizing the genuine warmth that hid beneath his stoic exterior. His raised fatty cheeks exposed a softer side reserved for those he held dear, such as Ricky, his son. It was a bright look packed with kindness and soundness, for it was a testament to the compassion he carried within him for those he truly cared for. "Before you leave the building, check on Jenni, please?" Unfit to challenge the former Sumo champion, Ricky bowed with regard for First Sergeant Kato.

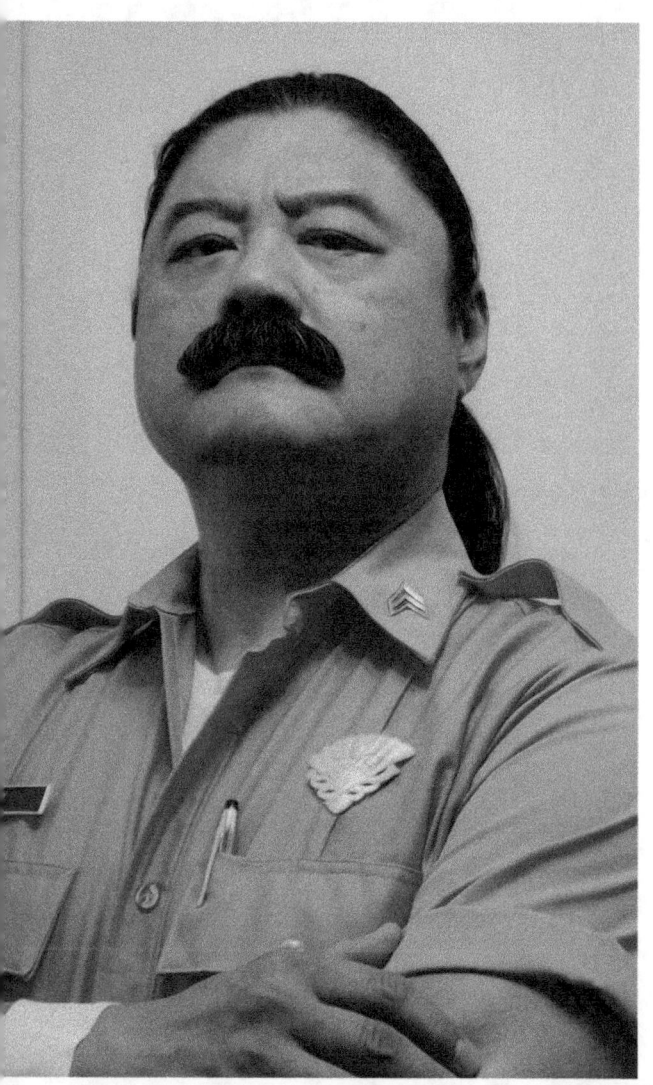

EAST FREELAND POLICE DEPARTMENT

54th

To: All Unity East Personnel
From: Captain Jenni
Subject: Commendation of First Sergeant's Leadership

Cadets,

I would like to formally recognize the exceptional leadership demonstrated by First Sergeant Kato in his role at Unity East. He has consistently exemplified Unity East's core values through his unwavering dedication to justice, compassion for our community, and innovative approach to law enforcement. Under First Sergeant Kato's leadership, Unity East has become a model precinct known for its unique blend of traditional values and modern policing techniques. Furthermore, his vision has allowed us to adapt to the ever-changing landscape of law enforcement while staying true to our commitment to serve and protect.

I encourage all personnel to reflect on First Sergeant Kato's instruction as his leadership continues to inspire us to strive for excellence in all aspects of our duties.

With determination and honor,
Captain Jenni

LESSONS IN HUMILITY

EAST FREELAND: ART STORY ONE

As the sun began its descent, Ricky's eyes widened in surprise as he felt his body hit the firm yet forgiving wooden foundation stretched out before him. The air rushed out of his lungs instantly, leaving him both breathless and beaten.

"Get up, big brother."

"Give me a moment, Captain." His ribs ached. He blinked twice, trying to process what had just happened. It was apparent that this wasn't the first fall during the session. Therefore, while reaching for his side, Ricky stole a moment to readjust his sunglasses before climbing to his feet.

Unity Martial Arts Center, the precinct's virtuous training dojo, was a spacious and well-equipped facility dedicated to developing Kato's police cadets' martial arts skills. Designed with functionality and traditional aesthetics in mind, it exuded an atmosphere of discipline, focus, and honor.

"Hurry!" she sounded.

LESSONS IN HUMILITY

Upon entering the magnificent dojo, one could be greeted by polished floors, an elevated platform, and a series of large mirrors mounted along one wall. Across from the reflective arrangement was a wide range of training equipment, including padded striking gear, boards for breaking, and sturdy wooden dummies for practicing knuckle strikes and turn kicks. Behind a swaying heavy bag, a weapons rack displayed an array of traditional martial arts weapons, such as wooden staffs, swords, and practice knives, highlighting the importance of weapon defense and control.

"Alright, already!" As he sought to reclaim his dignity, Ricky caught sight of Jenni's jet-black hair while she remained poised and composed in a kneeling position. "Why do you take training so seriously?" he asked. Her uniform, slightly worn but bearing the marks of countless hours of training, accentuated her serene presence on the thick padded mat from which he was thrown.

EAST FREELAND: ART STORY ONE

"Have you already forgotten Unity's code of conduct?" Hinting at Ricky's white sneakers, Jenni rigged her following words to tease him, for his shoes should have been removed and placed at the entry. "Silly brother, we who drill at Unity Martial Arts Center train barefooted to develop control over our movements, maintain a strong connection with the ground, and ensure stability and balance while performing combat techniques. Intimate contact with the training surface, such as the wooden floor, enhanced our ability to feel and respond to our opponent's movements."

"Of course, Captain, gosh."

Jenni's calm presentation suggested she could sense Ricky's conflicting beliefs. Similarly, her unwavering posture emanated resolve and control, contrasting sharply with her adopted brother's hardened nature.

"Strength alone is not enough to handle crime," she stated.

"Yeah? Then why did you embrace Aiki-

LESSONS IN HUMILITY

do?" Surveying her evident yet partial paralysis, Jenni thought over her evolving condition, which allowed her to move voluntarily without the assistance of her wheelchair.

"Aikido is not about overpowering your opponent. It's about using the opponent's energy against them while seeking balance amidst disorder. Just as in policing, it's not about brute force but finding peaceful solutions."

Realizing the significance of their sparring affair, Ricky swallowed his pride and slowly rose to his feet. The impact of Jenni's throw had shaken him to his core, not just physically but also mentally.

"I thought I could match your skill, but you've shown me otherwise, and for that, I am thankful, little sister."

Reflecting on his kind words, Jenni reduced her shoulders and turned to face him.

"It was a lesson I learned through my journey. My current physical condition forced me to find alternative ways to move and de-

EAST FREELAND: ART STORY ONE

fend myself. It taught me the value and the power of the mind."

"But how did you overcome that challenge? How did you find the strength to keep going?" Jenni's gaze was distant. Her memories nearly broke her. Nonetheless, she discovered the resilience to explore her challenging experience further.

"It wasn't easy, Ricky. There were moments when I felt defeated and I doubted myself. But I had a choice: either let my limitations define me or rise above them. So, I focused on what I could do rather than what I could not."

"I admire your determination, Jenni; I truly do. You've earned your role here as an essential cadet, and no one can take that away from you, not even me," he poked.

"Thank you, big brother, but remember; these lessons go beyond the mat. Policing requires the same resilience and courage, and always striving for righteousness while main-

LESSONS IN HUMILITY

taining respect for all." Ricky took a deep breath, released his balled-up fists, and found a cozy spot near Jenni to kneel.

"I'm trying to see the bigger picture, little sister."

Sensing Ricky's dismay, she reaches for his hand to bestow one last piece of wisdom.

"Together, big brother, we are formidable, but it is when you are alone, out there fighting the world, that I worry. Yet, I believe in your potential to evolve into a compassionate leader someday."

"Your guidance really packs a punch, Captain, but I am fully prepared to wholeheartedly embrace these lessons in humility," he declared with conviction.

"That's the spirit, Ricky!"

Her voice resonated against the backdrop of the setting sun, and as the day made way for nightfall, they solidified a profound bond, firmly grounded in joy and mutual respect, for it, was through this unbreakable connection

EAST FREELAND: ART STORY ONE

that they would continue to motivate each other, emerging as influential advocates in their quest for justice and harmony in East Freeland.

STREETS OF HARMONY

EAST FREELAND: ART STORY ONE

At the break of dawn, the city's citizens left their homes eager to grasp the many opportunities the new day had to offer. Pulsing with fresh energy, workers of all kinds moved with haste, and as the day progressed, so did the people of East Freeland.

From the highest peak of the slums, the Police Station Track could be seen, weaving its way through the urban terrain while connecting its residents to various destinations, both near and far.

As the whistling locomotive approached Unity East, the screeching noise of metal meeting metal announced its arrival, capturing the notice of onlookers lined up along the bay.

Police Station Track symbolized the interconnectedness of the people and the transient nature of life itself. It was a reminder that while Kato's cadets and their duty were rooted in the protection of the city, its heartbeat extended far beyond its boundaries, car-

STREETS OF HARMONY

ried by trains that came and went, accepting people from all walks of life.

The Metro Liner was especially vital to the sector as it stopped at various areas, taking after the cultural diversity within the urban sprawl.

The bus was wrapped in flashy colors with its route number prominently displayed, and as it steered through the neighborhood, its arrival was accompanied by a welcoming chime that beckoned passengers aboard.

The roads were adorned with signs written in Hangul, showcasing a community that had made its mark on the city. Meanwhile, various shops lined the route, offering a wide show of delicacies, products, and cultural experiences along the way.

But the metropole's trolley, Harmonious Journey with Ji-hoon, was the true symbol of unity and cultural fusion. Standing tall and proud, its emerald green exterior and golden accents honored the sun's warm glow, hint-

EAST FREELAND: ART STORY ONE

ing at the treasures waiting to be discovered. Hand-painted along its frame were elaborate symbols inspired by East Asian art, representing its commitment to sustainability, whereas decorated floral designs and delicate bamboo motifs added a touch of grace.

Inside, the trolley exuded a hospitable and tempting atmosphere. The wooden panels were buffed to a rich mahogany color for a much more cozy space for passengers. Moreover, its seating arrangements ensured that each passenger had a comfortable experience during their journey, while its accommodation allowed for a sense of intimacy and connection among the passengers, fostering a friendly and communal atmosphere as they explored the city together.

Among the numerous modes of transportation, "Harmonious Journey with Ji-hoon" was a sight that captured the imagination, beckoning all who witnessed it to embark on a remarkable adventure through the Streets

STREETS OF HARMONY

of Harmony.

Preparing for a long and eventful task ahead, a middle-aged man with a friendly face and a welcoming demeanor emerged, capturing the attention of passersby. His eyes sparkled with enthusiasm, signifying his genuine passion for his work.

Known for his likable optimism and an unyielding commitment to customer satisfaction, the kind-hearted individual deeply loved East Freeland and took great pride in showcasing its beauty and culture through the trolley experience.

Climbing into the driver's seat, the beloved owner and operator began to steer forward, and trailing behind him, like a jewel on wheels, was his green and golden trolley.

"Ladies and gentlemen, boys and girls, welcome aboard the Harmonious Journey! I am Ji-hoon Park, your guide and the proud owner of this magnificent trolley. Today, we embark on a remarkable adventure through

EAST FREELAND: ART STORY ONE

the echoing Streets of Harmony, where we will explore the richness that East Freeland has to offer." While Ji-hoon maneuvered the trolley through the happening routes, his voice, amplified by a handheld microphone, filled the coach through a well-placed speaker system. "Now, if you'll direct your attention to the handheld microphone in my hand, I will transport you to a world where the past and present harmoniously coexist. Picture the markets that once lined these same streets. The art, tantalizing aromas, and smiling faces filled the air. Ah, the memories! At each stop, we'll uncover their hidden echoes and pay tribute to the generations of this town's immigrants who sought new beginnings here."

HONK!

Amidst the rhythmic sound of the wheels rolling along the pavement, Ji-hoon wove a tale that spoke of the influential effect of his heritage and more.

HONK! HONK!

STREETS OF HARMONY

"As we journey through these Streets of Harmony, I'll share tales of the unified blend of East Freeland's cultural mix. You'll hear of the festivals that still resonate with joy, where the rhythmic beats of ancient drums intertwine with the laughter of families and friends that binds this town. With that, let your imagination soar as we relive these magnificent moments together."

DING!

"Look out the window, my friends, and marvel at the Korean-inspired architecture that dots our path. The intricate designs and elegant structures stand as a testament to the enduring legacy of Korea in East Freeland. There is so much to explore, so many hidden gems waiting to be discovered, and through my words and the sights before your eyes, I invite you to embrace the beauty of East Freeland's rich culture. Feel the connection, the unity that thrives within these streets."

Intertwined with the town's pulse, Ji-

EAST FREELAND: ART STORY ONE

hoon formed an authentic connection, understanding, and appreciation with his passengers, and along each passing landmark, he fostered a more profound sense of harmony and unity among all who called this side of Freeland home.

"So, my dear passengers, sit back, relax, and allow the Harmonious Journey to transport you through the Streets of Harmony, where the very greatness lives and breathes. Prepare to be captivated, inspired, and enlightened as we honor the spirited fusion that makes this town what it is today."

As the trolley continued its lyrical journey, Ji-hoon and his passengers further explored East Freeland, its treasured heritage, and the harmony that bound the remarkable city together.

#

Approaching the next stop, the bandaged

STREETS OF HARMONY

outsider clung to the alleyway when Ji-hoon's trolley drew near. But as the embarkees with sacks and luggage formed a line, a particular passenger caught the stranger's attention.

DING!

At the second clang of the trolley's bell, he watched the memorable passenger climb aboard with a hint of amusement creeping into his voice.

"A Cadet with a temper and the Inspector's fishy return…how convenient," he said before slipping away, leaving the faint scent of tobacco lingering in his absence.

ENTER THE INSPECTOR

ENTER THE INSPECTOR

Ji-hoon resumed his route, not before noticing a familiar figure among the passengers. While watching the road ahead, a hint of mystery about the rider suddenly sent a thrill through Ji-hoon, whom he identified as none other than the *Wanderer of Wonder*, known for his uncanny ability to unravel the most perplexing riddles, including ghost legends and forbidden magic.

"Inspector Wang, is that you?" Unable to contain the gladness within, Ji-hoon again announced the esteemed detective aboard the Harmonious Journey, "Eddie!" Seated calmly at the rear, the Inspector carefully surveyed the town with keen observation, magnified by spectacles resting on his nose beneath a fedora. "What an honor to have you aboard. Your reputation precedes you, and I must say, your presence adds an extra layer of mystery to our exploration of East Freeland's secrets." The passengers nearby then shifted their attention, delighted by the unexpected meeting

EAST FREELAND: ART STORY ONE

between the operator and the Inspector.

"Thank you, thank you," smiled the Inspector. Gesturing toward an empty seat near the front of the trolley, Ji-hoon invited Eddie to join him.

"Please, take a seat, Inspector," he said, his voice filled with excitement and curiosity. "Allow me to continue my tales, and perhaps, together, we can unlock the hidden truths that reside within these streets." Eddie humbly obliged, settling into the seat with a sense of gratitude.

"Thank you again, Mr. Park." Touches of a mystical past glimmered from the Inspector's jade-adorned wrist, while his long gray coat formed a harmonious blend of traditional Eastern themes and modern Western cuts, symbolizing his role as a cultural bridge in this setting.

"It was my pleasure, Inspector."

As the trolley gracefully glided through the city, Ji-hoon couldn't help but wonder

ENTER THE INSPECTOR

what mysteries the Inspector would uncover during their shared voyage. What secrets lay hidden amidst the patchwork of East Freeland? Little did they know that this chance encounter onboard the trolley set a chain of events in motion that would lead them on a thrilling adventure through the mysterious streets.

With each passing landmark, Eddie's presence completed Ji-hoon's vivid storytelling until their journey through the Streets of Harmony neared its conclusion, and as the trolley came to a gentle halt, he and Ji-hoon Park exchanged a knowing glance of admiration and gratitude.

"I'll be seeing you, Mr. Park." Ready to disembark the Harmonious Journey, Eddie made his way towards the exit when Ji-hoon's voice reverberated through the trolley.

"Inspector! Before you go, may I introduce you to a special companion who has joined us on our journey?" Suddenly, a smile

EAST FREELAND: ART STORY ONE

played on his lips as Eddie's curiosity piqued. Hence, the Inspector awaited the introduction until an undersized, neglected stray emerged from beneath one of the seats.

"What is this?" Eddie's eyes softened as he crouched down to extend a welcoming hand to be explored.

"His name is Kenji, Inspector," said Ji-hoon.

He was especially pleased to see the town's stray take to someone well respected in East Freeland. It was as if the universe had aligned to unite these two, destined to become companions on their respective journeys.

"And it seems our paths have crossed at just the right moment," Eddie spoke. "How about you join me to unravel East Freeland's mysteries that await us?"

Kenji's enthusiasm lit up like a seasonal firecracker as if he understood the invitation and eagerly accepted it. Thus, Eddie's heart

ENTER THE INSPECTOR

swelled with a newfound sense of companionship, and with a final nod of appreciation to Ji-hoon and the other passengers, Eddie and Kenji stepped off the trolley and into the streets.

Eventually, the two approached a small eatery found just a stone's throw away from the trolley's finishing stop and welcomed by the aroma of sizzling bulgogi wafting through the air.

"Well, my new friend, shall we indulge in some sustenance?" Eddie glanced down at Kenji, who wagged his tail in like-mindedness.

The restaurant's exterior appeared meek but welcoming. However, as they approached the doorway, the Inspector noticed a small "No Dogs Allowed" sign hanging in the window.

"Ah, what a predicament," Eddie mused, stroking his chin thoughtfully. "Stay…I'll only be but a moment," said the Inspector as

EAST FREELAND: ART STORY ONE

he pushed open the door.

Stepping into a modest restaurant, Eddie removed his hat, revealing his eyes as they drifted to a faded wooden banner above the kitchen that proudly proclaimed the establishment: Humble Rice House.

The interior exuded a nostalgic charm. The walls were adorned with weathered calendars showcasing breathtaking landscapes decorated with the elegant strokes of Hangul. Overhead, the warm glow of scattered bulbs cast a gentle light on a sea of worn wooden tables and chairs while the rhythmic hum of a ceiling fan stirred the aroma of home-cooked meals throughout the business.

"Annyeonghaseyo!"

Sharp and observant, Eddie's face bore the marks of wisdom and experience, but a softness resonated within him. Despite his formal attire, an old leather satchel filled with medical supplies and ancient texts on martial arts and immortality hinted at his role as a

ENTER THE INSPECTOR

healer, perhaps possessing intricate knowledge of the human body.

"Annyeonghaseyo!" he replied.

Emerging from the kitchen, two elderly cooks, well in their sixties, welcomed the investigator with honor while introducing themselves as the proud owners of the long-standing establishment.

"Welcome back, Inspector. How may we serve you this fine morning?" said the kind man while his spouse, rather thoughtfully, reached for utensils and napkins.

"Ah, a bowl of sticky rice, a side of kimchi, and a steamy kettle of hot loose-leaf tea will do." The owners nodded, assuring him that his request would be promptly fulfilled.

"Of course, Inspector."

NOTHING OR DOUBLE

NOTHING OR DOUBLE

Leaving the Humble Rice House, Eddie bid the couple a fond farewell and summoned Kenji from the steps out front. Ever the sightseer, he scouted their next course and entered the street only to be drawn away to the airy exuberance of Oriental Town Market.

"Are you ready for another adventure, Kenji?" he asked. Thus, his animal companion mirrored his next steps in the direction of O-Town.

Flickering lanterns dangling overhead lit the busy pathway to a collective of stalls decorated in deep fabrics and detailed embellishments. Meanwhile, the evening breeze intermingled with the expectations of cheerful festivity carried the aroma of exotic spices and blazing street food among many offerings.

Amidst the sea of commerce, their voices rang out, enticing customers with enthusiastic gestures and persuasive expressions, and where bargaining and laughter commixed as the market became a stirring hub of inter-

EAST FREELAND: ART STORY ONE

action and exchange. O-Town was not just a place of transaction but also a treasure trove of information.

As he and Kenji ventured deeper into the heart of the market, Eddie observed the subtle nuances of exchanges, catching snippets of rumors and whispers that hinted at a hidden corner tucked away from the main thoroughfare. Thus, the two pressed onwards.

Nestled beyond the arresting red Z6-R parked behind a cluster of splintered crates, Eddie spotted a crowd gathered around two players seated at a worn makeshift gambling dice table with one being a familiar face from Unity East.

"Ricky?"

Choosing to remain an observer, Eddie found a nearby stall to lean against while Kenji rested his furry rear, where he studied the game's dynamics and the strategies and probabilities at play. He took notice of each onlooker, distinctive in appearance, as they

NOTHING OR DOUBLE

brought their own mannerisms to the table, alluding to the complex jumble of lives that led them to this underground den of gambling.

Sitting across from Ricky was a beefy man, enriched with thick arms and calloused hands betraying a life of hard labor. His face was etched with a deep scowl that framed his beady eyes as he watched the cop's every move, searching for any sign of deception.

As the dice clattered across the table, he'd grunt and curse with each roll that favored Ricky, while his pudgy fingers would fold into fists as he struggled to maintain his composure.

On the other hand, Ricky remained unshakable, and his movements were both fluid and precise. He would occasionally flash a cocky grin, cheering in his opponent's growing frustration, for his efforts were fueled by his uncanny ability to read the subtle patterns and nuances of the game.

But at this moment of observance, Ed-

EAST FREELAND: ART STORY ONE

die's role transcended that of a mere detective, gathering details on Ricky and the participants encircling him. It was a glimpse into the depths of human complexity, a reminder that even those tasked with upholding the law could be entangled in the allure of forbidden pursuits.

Unlike the other players, Ricky didn't rely solely on luck or blind chance. His strategy, honed through years of policing and martial arts, involved a combination of controlled throws and strategic betting. He would carefully adjust his grip on the dice, applying just the right amount of force to achieve the desired outcome.

As the dice clattered against the wooden surface, Ricky's winning streak began to draw attention and envy following whispers of conspiracy and foul play, gradually transforming into a wave of simmering bitterness. Meanwhile, Eddie noticed this not before the brute, who couldn't contain his suspicions any

NOTHING OR DOUBLE

longer, slammed his fist on the game's surface, causing the dice to roll aimlessly off the table.

BAM!

"Something's not right here!" he bellowed. "Ricky...you're cheating!"

However, as the tension escalated, Ricky wedged a crinkled cigarette between his teeth, and with a willful motion, he reached into the innermost pocket of his rugged leather jacket.

"Hold on."

Eyeing Ricky's hand, the brute speaks on a law known throughout the town.

"Guns are banned in this town, Ricky, don't forget."

Yet, Rick's search continued until he recovered the article and placed it on the table for all to see, even the Inspector.

SLAM!

The unruly crowd suddenly fell into an uneasy silence, realizing the precarious position they now found themselves in.

EAST FREELAND: ART STORY ONE

"I should take you all in for illegal gambling in O-Town!" Ricky shouted. The badge, a symbol of his position within Unity East, served as a warning, demanding respect with caution at once. "That's what I thought," he said. His conduct was aggressive and rather impulsive, as it became clear that Ricky wasn't merely another bettor at the table but an individual who had pledged to safeguard East Freeland by enforcing the law.

Accordingly, the gambler and his pose, realizing the implications of their shiftings, stepped away from the table, and as for Ricky, he no longer faced the accusations that threatened to disrupt the harmony of the market.

"I never thought I'd find you here, engaged in a game like this, especially as an authorized peace keeper."

"Inspector?" Ricky's voice carried a tone of familiarity while his eyes flickered with a combination of guilt and defiance, for he was found in a compromising situation that

NOTHING OR DOUBLE

could potentially jeopardize his position within Unity East.

"As an officer of the law, engaging in illegal gambling compromises your integrity and the trust the department places on you. We have a responsibility to uphold the law, not to break it."

"Oh c'mon, Wang…it's just a game."

"Policing this town is a serious matter, one that should not be taken lightly, particularly under the watchful eye of First Sergeant Kato," the Inspector cautioned. "His reputation for uncompromising enforcement of the law is well-known, and any misstep on your part could have grave consequences for your career and the public's trust in the police force."

"Yeah, yeah, yeah, so did you come back to O-Town just to lecture me, or are you looking to walk away with some of these winnings?" With the others gone, the gambler's burrow has become Ricky's stage.

EAST FREELAND: ART STORY ONE

"In truth, Ricky, I'm—"

"Nothing or double?" Ricky's dare cut through the background bluster with assured finality, and surprisingly, Eddie's lips parted slightly, betraying his stance on the scandalous cop's dirty-dealing pastime.

"What did you have in mind?"

As Ricky rose from the table, he finished a glass catch of scorched rice water, emptying it in one fluid motion.

"If I can cut through this bottle with my bare hand, you must promise never to lecture me about duty and integrity ever again. But—if I fail, I'll open myself up to your guidance and support in overcoming my gambling habit."

Intrigued by Ricky's proposal both Eddie and Kenji raised an eyebrow. Although poached with skepticism, Eddie nodded, accepting the challenge.

"Very well, Ricky."

With that, Ricky struck the table with

NOTHING OR DOUBLE

competitive readiness.

"You're on, Wang!"

Positioning the empty vessel at the center of the dice table, Ricky assumed a resolute stance, preparing himself mentally and physically for the friendly wager. Then, with a quick action too swift to follow, his knife hand slashed through the air, aimed to split the bottle with the force of his determination and conviction.

But as the edge of his palm struck the glass vessel, a burst of force erupted from the impact, causing it to rebound off the table and, in an unanticipated development, hurtle towards Eddie at a startling rate.

Just the same, the Inspector's hand shot out, snatching the erring object mid-flight, only to place the unscathed bottle back on the table.

"Perhaps it's time to reconsider your understanding behind such wagers, Ricky," he said reasonably but not unkind.

EAST FREELAND: ART STORY ONE

Floored by the realization that the bottle didn't break, Ricky's eyes widened, with his bargain to Eddie dawning upon him.

"It always worked for Jackie."

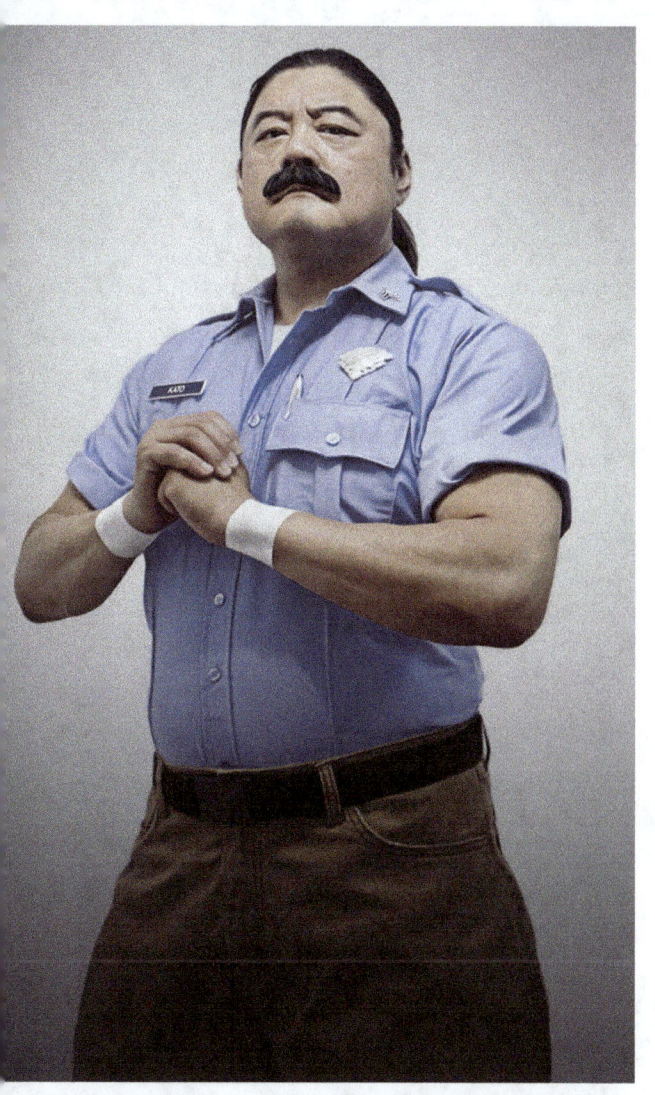

HI-YA!

First Sergeant Kato, the towering pillar of Unity East, commands respect with his stoic presence, unmatched fighting abilities, and unwavering dedication to justice. Once a professional sumo wrestler, he now leads East Freeland's most compassionate police agency with the same headstrong attitude and imposing size, while showcasing his formidable skills to uphold the law.

WEAKNESS

Despite his strength and leadership, Kato's greatest weakness lies in his stubborn adherence to tradition. His resistance to modern policing methods, particularly his aversion to firearms, can sometimes put his cadets at a tactical disadvantage in dangerous situations.

FUN FACT

Beneath his tough exterior, Kato maintains a small collection of meticulously pruned plants, using the art of bonsai as a metaphor for shaping and guiding his cadets' growth and development.

HI-YA!

Ricky, Unity East's heroic police cadet, patrols the beat of East Freeland with unwavering dedication. His mastery of Karate and skilled use of the single tonfa make him a formidable force against crime. Driven by a desire for justice and haunted by his past, Ricky's journey from a bullied child to a respected guardian is a testament to his passion for protecting the innocent by becoming the Tornado of Justice.

WEAKNESS

Ricky's greatest weakness lies in his quick temper. His childhood experiences of discrimination have left him with emotional scars that sometimes cloud his judgment, leading to impulsive decisions. This rashness puts him at odds with his colleagues and even his investigations.

FUN FACT

Despite his explosive temper, Ricky is an enthusiastic fan of martial arts films, particularly those produced by East Freeland's own Soaring Pictures.

HI-YA!
Jung, the ruthless and complex leader of the 7 Streeters, rules the streets of East Freeland with an iron fist. Driven by anger and a thirst for control, reinforced by his mastery of the lethal nunchaku and Taekwondo, Jung's rise to prominence in the criminal hierarchy stands as a reminder of his uncompromising ambition and strategic brilliance.

WEAKNESS
Jung's greatest weakness lies beneath his tough exterior. His drug addiction, meant to boost his fighting skills, now hurts his health and leadership. This habit causes problems within the 7 Streeters, as Jung's behavior becomes unpredictable.

FUN FACT
Heedless of his battle with addiction, Jung harbors a secret love for classic rock music, a remnant of his bond with Ricky.

CONTRABAND

EAST FREELAND: ART STORY ONE

As the day drew to a close, the market's lively vibrance gradually gave way to a rising sense of unease that overshadowed the mighty spirit of O-Town. The rich aroma of delectable fare and merry merchant laughter that flooded the streets was suddenly overtaken by the stuffy stench of motor oil and roaring engines, earning the notice of one reckless Cadet and the wandering Inspector.

"7 Streeters."

"I'm sorry, come again?"

The 7 Streeters' arrival was a clear sign of trouble. Their notorious reputation for illegal dealings and causing harm was just enough for a hero to step in. Thus, as the gang began to make their move, most held their breath while others looked away, and as for Ricky—

"Wait here, Inspector."

"Right." As advised, Eddie and Kenji both stood back, allowing Ricky to pursue the gang as they entered the Bidder's Den, a shady crossing where the underbelly of East

CONTRABAND

Freeland came to life. "It has begun."

Ricky found his footing down a weird aisle that led underground to a destination where only the forbidden were welcomed.

Once inside, Ricky found several tables tagged with stolen art and antiquities, rare animal skins, and counterfeit alcohol and tobacco products that bypassed taxes and the city's fixed regulations.

Exploring the scene from corner to corner, he eventually spotted the suspicious pack of bikers staging their products before a suit-clad businessman, seemingly capable by all appearances, suggesting he was no stranger to clandestine dealings.

"Anything here can be yours for a price," the dealer proclaimed. The glimmer of his golden additions, unveiled beneath the warm bulbs of the illicit enclosure, foreshadowed a figure who personified an ostentatious lifestyle; may it all have been achieved through illegal means.

EAST FREELAND: ART STORY ONE

"Dealing with 7 Streeters now, Benny?" he countered. Ricky could sense the underlying suspicion bleeding through the hustler's gold-toothed grin, a barbaric reminder that trust was a rare and valuable commodity in the shadows of the Bidder's Den.

"Shit."

"Yo, Benny!" one of the seven invited, ready to strike a deal. "Are we doing this or not?"

"Certainly!" Benny was a man of many words and even more secrets. "Hear me out, Ricky," he pleaded. "This isn't my deal…t-they just showed up, I swear!" But then, as their exchange gradually waned, Ricky witnessed the 7 Streeters uncovering firearm after firearm for trade amidst the Den's random circus.

"You just found yourself in deep water," declared Ricky. Then, shoving the golden dealer aside, he sprinted toward the surface topped with handguns and ammunition, and

CONTRABAND

as he closed in on the 7 Streeters, the brash cadet lifted his heel high above his head and brought down an unlawful axe kick, splitting their station into two jagged halves.

CRASH!

Ricky's discovery of firearms was all the proof he needed to convince Kato of the 7 Streeters' growing hold over the town, and as the bikers found their footing, the daring cadet dove into action, crashing into them with enough might to bust their defenses.

WHAM—WHAM—CRACK!

Ricky moved like a whirlwind, delivering kick after kick while his knees found their mark, opening up opportunities to press his advantage in a brutal symphony of violence.

WHAM—WHAM—SMASH!

Driven by a burning obsession to shatter their operation, he became the unstoppable Tornado of Justice, and as for the 7 Streeters, for all their bravado and swagger, they became mere obstacles in his path, to be swept

EAST FREELAND: ART STORY ONE

aside like leaves fallen from a tree.

Meanwhile, the Inspector, despite being left behind, was far from inactive, for he had a knack for blending into the scene, thus making him a silent spectator amidst the disarray. He was fixed on Ricky's commitment as he fought with the same fire that often burned in others who sought to make a difference, and as he continued to observe, he neglected to warn him of a key figure whose actions would shift the course of this story.

"Who else wants to go to jail?" Ricky's leather jacket swished through the air as he sent a 7 Streeter across the room by the force of a brutish storm kick.

WHAM!

Rushing in like a sparkling bottle rocket, another attacker threatened to stop the fighting cadet, only to be floored with a brutal onslaught of bone-breaking punches following a spinning elbow to his skull.

CRUNCH!

CONTRABAND

Watching from a tricky vantage point, Benny's golden chains, glinting under the low light, gave him away as he witnessed Ricky dismantle the 7 Streeters, one biker after the next.

"Stay down," Ricky growled. But then, a razor-sharp clicking noise, reminiscent of a weapon being primed, disrupted the encounter.

CLICK—CLACK!

The sliding sound of metal against metal was unmistakable. Everyone in attendance, including Ricky, remained motionless, for he, above the rest, had been compromised.

"You should've stayed out of this, Mr. Policeman."

The skin stretching across Ricky's knuckles grew tense while his eyes flashed behind the innermost corner of his shady shades.

"Drop the piece, asshole," he warned.

Minutes seemed to stall as the gunman's outstretched arm and weapon were aimed

EAST FREELAND: ART STORY ONE

directly at the rear of Ricky's head while Benny knew all too well the consequences of breaking the law set forth by Unity East, but the prospect of betraying the 7 Streeters was equally terrifying.

"You cannot stop what's coming."
BANG!

EAST FREELAND POLICE DEPARTMENT

54th

To: First Sergeant Kato
From: Captain Jenni
Subject: Ricky's Conduct

Father,

Before addressing Ricky's conduct, it's crucial to understand the complexity of his character. His experiences with both loss and discrimination have molded him into a determined but often aggressive cadet. Ricky's tendency to make hasty judgments stem from deeply rooted internal struggles, particularly concerning his brother's involvement in criminal activities. While his commitment to combating crime is undeniable, Ricky's propensity for violence and his rebellious streak have made him a divisive presence within our ranks. His methods, though effective at times, frequently clash with our department's standards and values.

With determination and honor,
Captain Jenni

UNITY SHAKEN

EAST FREELAND: ART STORY ONE

As the mantle of darkness cloaked all of Freeland City, Ricky stormed through the glass doors of Unity East, hauling a crook in handcuffs.

Positioned strategically at the juncture leading to the rest of the precinct's departments stood First Sergeant Kato, arms folded, for he had eyes and ears all over, and when Ricky caused trouble, he was always the first to hear about it.

"You'd better have a good explanation for bringing Min Jae-ho into my domain without due cause?" Despite Kato's demanding tone, Ricky's attitude masked behind his dark shades, crinkled with defiance and a hint of an untold narrative.

"I apprehended this weasel trading contraband in O-Town," he reported.

Wheeling down the hall from her office, Jenni finally arrived to find Ricky and her father in the heat of an intense exchange of honor, courage, and accountability.

UNITY SHAKEN

"And what were you doing down there exactly?"

"Father," Jenni had put wised.

"You were over there gambling again, weren't you?"

"Father, please," she begged, pleading for her father's understanding. Yet, he ignored her and to Ricky's surprise, Kato was onto him as though he could see straight past the sunglasses covering his eyes.

"What does it matter anyway, huh?" Having felt slighted by Kato's accusations, Ricky reached into his jacket to regain a shred of chilling evidence from his rumble at the Bidder's Den. "See this weapon? I confiscated it from the 7 Streeters dealing in the den," he announced.

"What is this, Benny?" Kato demanded.

"Care to explain," Ricky taunted.

"What does this even mean…how did that find its way into our city?" Jenni wondered aloud. But Benny, who had been silent

EAST FREELAND: ART STORY ONE

throughout the debate, finally spoke up.

"I didn't want to go through with the deal, but if he thinks I was behind this, I'm dead."

"He's lying!" Ricky shouted. His patience was waning, but not his fists; they could fight 7 Streeters all night if they had to.

"That's enough," Kato interjected, "We'll keep you safe," he proposed, but as he began to outline further directives—

"That's a Norinco Type 54. It was manufactured in 1973, also known as the Chinese Tokarev," Jenni exposed. "Based off of the absent emblem, and aged metal, it had to have been imported from across the sea. But that could only mean one thing."

"Please! Lock me up, I beg you. I'm a marked man out there!" Benny attested. But Ricky wasn't going for it as he spoke against him.

"Shut up!"

"Ricky, relinquish that weapon," Kato intervened. "We must adhere to the rules and

UNITY SHAKEN

evaluate the situation before initiating any further action."

"No!" he bellowed. His voice had an uneven edge that underlined his resolve, clearly perceived by everyone present at the station after nightfall. "7 Streeters are a danger to this city, and I'm going to confront them tonight, alone if I have to!"

"Ricky, you can't just go off on your own like this."

"Jenni's right, Ricky," Kato expressed in agreement. "Your proposed course of action carries considerable risk, and I will not allow it."

"I'm taking this gun, and I'm taking Benny with me to show them that they are not above the law!"

"Absolutely not!" Kato shouted. "This is not how we operate at Unity East, Benny stays here, and that's an order!"

"Oh, thank you, Captain Kato," Benny pleaded with great depth and desperation.

EAST FREELAND: ART STORY ONE

"It's First Sergeant, you big dummy," Jenni corrected.

"Right...King Kato—"

"Enough of this already!" Reaching his limit, Ricky's final words of warning echoed throughout the precinct, hinting at a game of death on the rise. "After tonight, the 7 Streeters will be no more," he declared, and so, with the handgun in his possession, Ricky abandoned Kato, Jenni, and Benny and forcefully exited Unity East to pursue a matter that could no longer be forgiven.

DEFYING KATO'S ORDERS

EAST FREELAND: ART STORY ONE

The sportcar's tires gripped the slick asphalt with a defiant tenacity, propelling Ricky ever closer to his next and final destination. The unforgiving rain beating against the windshield only amplified his escalating determination, and as the car's speedometer needle crept higher and higher, Freeland's mega harbor came into view.

Seeking retribution behind a firm grasp over the steering wheel, Ricky couldn't suppress the deafening replay of gunfire at point-blank range, which further encouraged him to face the 7 Streeters on their own turf, even if it meant defying First Sergeant's orders.

As the racing machine's headlamps exposed the dockyard, Ricky whipped the Z6-R to a skidding halt and vaulted out to lay eyes on a wide archway marked by a sign that read Ocean Bounty Bazaar: The Largest Seaport in Freeland City. Back at the precinct, he had made a commitment to end the 7 Streeters, and that night, as he stood before the gang's

DEFYING KATO'S ORDERS

stronghold, he was bent on bringing them down for good.

Keying the lock to his trunk, Ricky lifted the car panel to expose Kato's Nightstick, or his Single-Handed Rebel as he now called it—a rigid, cranium-crushing Tonfa that rested next to his sole detainee, who had been bruised, distressed, and restrained with handcuffs. But although Ricky had handed Min Jae-ho over to Kato earlier, he was unwilling to spare the shooter, for he had other plans.

"Get out."

The path through the bazaar was a chaotic maze, swarming with makeshift booths, clattering knives, and the haggling voices of those who could be hiding something far more sinister than what was sold at the dockyard's Seaport Seafood Haven, and Ricky knew it.

Maneuvering through the shouting voices of fishmongers and the mucky spills of the gutting of sea life caught just beyond the

EAST FREELAND: ART STORY ONE

wooden planks beneath their feet, the reek of the brine from the day's open catch struck Ricky's prisoner, driving him to vomit all over his shoes.

"Oh, c'mon!" he shouted. But then, with a forceful grip—

CRUNCH!

"ARGH!"

"Where is he?" Ricky demanded, having twisted the gunman's wrist past its limit.

"The disco…just beyond that point," he confessed.

Suddenly, Ricky's fist flexed in utter hatred, foretelling a personal confrontation that awaited him upon speaking two words.

"Hate Club."

Looking ahead, the daring policeman set his sights on a colossal neon sign luring partygoers into the active venue while Freeland's graffiti-riddled metro rumbled above it.

"If he's here, he would be there…he's always there," muttered the shooter.

DEFYING KATO'S ORDERS

With that, Ricky pressed forward, shoving his prisoner ahead in a way that drew the curiosity of prying eyes narrowing at the sight of Ricky's unmistakable leather jacket and the bound criminal before him.

"Move it."

#

Materializing from the mist beyond the bazaar, the bandaged outsider tracked Ricky's relentless march toward the club, unnoticed by the spattering rain.

Meanwhile, passersby, sensing the non-native's unsettling presence joined by a wooden bokken at his side, quickened their pace, adding to the mounting suspense throughout the dockyard.

"Perfect…the stage is now set for chaos."

HATE CLUB

HATE CLUB

Entering the disco, the cadet and his suspect were greeted by the cacophony of hyperactive music, live nudity, and the fleeting glimpses of those lost in ecstasy, exposed beneath a dazzling array of neon pink, electric blue, and fiery violet hues reeling overhead.

The air was stagnant, tainted with sweat and booze, but as they pushed deeper into the heart of Hate Club, the active mass of revelers made a path for them, unveiling a vast expanse of polished black tiles that seemed to throb with the thunderous bassline. It was here where the energy of the crowd reached its feverish apex. But this only sickened Ricky, and if it weren't for the task at hand, he would have rounded up everyone under the influence and stuffed them in a cage at Unity East. And so, he sent the prisoner skidding across the slick surface of the dance floor and into the disco's sound booth.

CRASH!

"I'm looking for someone!" Ricky's voice

EAST FREELAND: ART STORY ONE

cut through the DJ's record, leaving an eerie silence in its wake. "Anybody seen Jung?" The crowd's movement stilled, giving way to him as the solo force that he was. "The man I'm looking for is bony, bald, and hates wearing shoes because he thinks he can kick his way out of trouble, which, I suppose, makes him a real badass!" Ricky's tone leaked with mockery, but still, not a flicker even crossed their faces. But then, recalling the wager he had lost at O-Town, Ricky selected a nearby table, and with the same knife hand he entrusted to break the scorched rice water bottle, he separated the drink rest with one mightful strike.

SMASH!

"Are you all fucking deaf?" he barked. But as if bullying the crowd wasn't enough, Ricky's rampage continued as he kicked at another table, this time splattering liquor on a gorgeous group of women modeling the latest fashion trend in Freeland City. But he didn't care. His tactics were designed to create chaos until someone—anyone—cracked. "Somebody better start talking."

Losing patience, Ricky delved into his coat anew, and, with a frustrated huff, he rummaged around his badge, a crumpled sales slip, and a crumpled pack of creased cigarettes before finally closing around what he sought after—

BLAM! BLAM! BLAM!

"Do I have everyone's attention now?" The gunfire drew gasps from several witnesses, and as whispers began to spread, one man finally stepped forward.

"It's just one guy with one gun trying to scare us all." The crowd's murmur intensified, but Ricky remained steadfast behind any indication of uncertainty. "Can't you see beyond those cheap sunglasses of yours?" he jeered. "We're 7 Streeters!" Thus, sensing an opportunity for entertainment, the gathering erupted into laughter only to detect no fear and only judgment.

EAST FREELAND: ART STORY ONE

"You look like a smart man," Ricky started, "I'm a cop, you know."

"So why don't you turn around before things get bad for you?" Amused with the cocky street thug, Ricky's grip on the gun tightened as he stepped forward.

"Perhaps I've been looking for the wrong person all along, and just maybe…this gun belongs to you." Like a good joke gone wrong, the laughter ceased as tension crystallized around them. The 7 Streeter, too, faltered as if Ricky's accusation fit the bill. Hence, signaling others to join him, four more members arose from the crowd, forming a loose semicircle around Ricky. "Oh, I see, you must be some kind of high-ranking tough guy…can you fight?"

"Yeah—I bet I could rip those fancy shades right off that pretty face of yours before you can say another word," claimed the 7 Streeter, cracking his knuckles under the sudden hush that had fallen over the disco. Yet,

HATE CLUB

the tinted eyewear Ricky sported concealed not just his daring stare but a multitude of emotions, but even a tinge of pity for the misguided fool standing in front of him, for silly threats meant little in his world of police work.

"Listen up! I'm not here to start a war; I'm here to confront a guy who has a fishhook pierced through his lip, and that's all." His stubborn gaze swept over the faces in the crowd, each one reflecting varying degrees of suspicion and heedfulness.

"Hey! We're not done talking!" yelled the 7 Streeter. However, Ricky was unfazed by the bruiser's empty threats, for he was very intentional about his pursuit within Hate Club.

"How about you step aside before I shake down this entire scene, starting with you."

The 7 Streeter's reaction was instantaneous. His eyes widened in shock, and his fist intensified with outrage, and for a split second, it seemed he would lash out. But before he could attempt to do so, another man's voice

EAST FREELAND: ART STORY ONE

halted him in place.

"Stop!"

Surrounded by a squad of suspicious individuals dressed in graphic hoodies, loose sweatpants, and white high-top sneakers on their feet with their motorcycle visors flipped up, a bald and bare-footed character lounging arrogantly in his martial arts uniform on a makeshift throne amidst a thick haze of marijuana smoke, fixed his gaze upon the brazen cadet as if he had known him for decades.

"Jung," Ricky disclosed, identifying the leader of the 7 Streeters just as he had described. The smirk that had graced his face moments earlier vanished, replaced by a steely resolve, and as the room shrunk, their conflicting paths finally intersected with words that transcended mere legalities.

"How dare you come into my establishment, assault my guests, and threaten the lives of my friends with a gun in your hand? It's beneath you, Ricky." Jung's fraying uniform was

HATE CLUB

a symbol that evoked fear and respect among his devoted followers as it was a embroidering of battles fought and victories claimed, along with several patches, each collected over time as a formative student, woven into the very fabric of his legend.

At that very moment, Ricky refused to be shamed by the street king's chastising statement. Therefore, he stood rooted and undivided in the center of Hate Club.

"You don't want me showing up, that's fair, but a gun washed up on my turf, which means your business is now my business."

"You have your side, Ricky…don't tell me how to run mine," Jung replied.

"Yeah, and yet, you see everything that enters and exits this town by sea, but somehow you missed this one didn't you?" Ricky expressed, dangling the weapon before him. His remark struck home for Jung, noticed by his hands clenched around the armrests of his chair. Nonetheless, he didn't take the bait. Instead, he reclined with a cunning smile playing on his lips, just as any crime lord would do in the face of the law.

"You've always been good at playing policeman, haven't you?" Following that remark, Jung's grin widened into a taunting sneer as he shook his head slowly in exaggerated disappointment. "Well, now that you're here, and it doesn't look like you're leaving without the truth, how about we square up, your fists against my kicks?"

"Let's go, asshole!" oK'd the cop lord, and then, with a daring challenge squeezing the stage, the onlookers held their breath as the anticipation reached its—

"HOA!"

Jung exploded from his throne with a soaring kick, a deceitful technique that was destructive as it was inescapable. Just the same, Ricky removed his shades and braced himself at the last possible second to allow the brunt of Jung's heel to deflect harmlessly off his shoulder.

WHAM!

"Argh—is that all you've got!" Ricky taunted, not before placing his sunglasses over his eyes. Meanwhile, the crowd of spectators, including the 7 Streeters, who had been so eager to challenge Ricky moments earlier, quickly retreated to the edges of the room.

Gaining new ground, Jung launched his bare feet in ways that seemed to defy the laws of physics.

WHOOSH! WHOOSH! WHOOSH—WHOOSH!

"You shouldn't have come here," Threatened Jung. But Ricky, sharp but wary, parried each kick with well-timed precision, knowing each foot hurled could grant the gangster a fatal advantage.

"And you should lay off the drugs," Ricky gritted out, and as the fight revealed the next opening, he seized it with a mighty punch to end Jung's wrath.

EAST FREELAND: ART STORY ONE

WHAM!

"Argh—have you forgotten what we were, Ricky?"

"I'm not the one who's bent on tearing us apart, Jung."

Then, as the battle reached its climax, a sudden commotion at the entrance drew everyone's lookout.

SMASH!

"This is the police!"

Falling in one after another, a team of armed cadets, led by First Sergeant Kato, stormed into the nightspot with enough weapons to shut down the entire harbor.

"It's past active hours here at Hate Club—NOW BEAT IT!" Kato's booming presence was neither good for Ricky nor Jung and as for the crowd of onlookers, they scattered in fear, forced out by the police. "And you two," Kato began, "this is not the way," he said firmly but not unfriendly. "For heaven's sake, you should be standing together, not tearing each other apart!"

At that particular moment, Ricky and Jung exchanged glances filled with bitterness, pain, and something much deeper.

"But father, if only you could see what I see, Jung's a thug—a disgrace, and even worse, he's a danger to this family!"

"And you're a cadet, Ricky—Freeland's symbol of justice and order, why don't you act like one!" Kato gainsaid. "And Jung," he continued, "what have you been up to lately? Stealing cars, extorting Mr. Ko, huh—smoking dope? I'm the top watchman of this town, and this is how you embarrass me, huh? What do you have to say for yourself?"

Kato's mighty words echoed in the empty disco, and as for Jung, his emotions appeared to shift between resentment and a deep-seated vulnerability. Moreover, his gaze flickered with a hint of shame, as if the weight of his father's disappointment had managed to penetrate his hardened exterior.

EAST FREELAND: ART STORY ONE

"You two may not have faith in me, but I'm good at some things, you know," Jung started. "Look around, old man—I've made a name for myself!" However, that fleeting moment of defenselessness quickly dissipated, replaced by a cold resolve that masked any lingering doubts or regrets. Thus, Jung exploded. "But you know what, I don't need your approval, I've got a reputation to uphold now because I'm a fucking 7 Streeter!"

"No, you're not dammit! You have a family already, Jung! Ricky's still your brother, and you're my son!"

"No he's not father!"

"Shut it, Ricky!" shouted Kato, "You've already caused enough trouble for one night," he divulged, along with a long-winded lecture to follow. "You two are what Freeland City requires, but neither of you can do it alone. You'll need each other because you're bound by blood, nothing more and nothing less."

Considering Kato's message, Ricky ex-

HATE CLUB

amined the Chinese pistol and, with a profound sigh, released it over to Kato.

"I'm done with this," he expressed.

"And?" Kato implied, motioning at the other.

"And I was wrong in accusing you of such things, Jung. Will you forgive me?" he asked. Ricky's gesture appeased the commanding officer in charge, whereupon he then faced Jung with an invitation to correct their disagreements in a manner that only a nurturing parent would.

"Will you choose to stand with him now, my son?" asked First Sergeant Kato. Yet, Jung was speechless. He couldn't find the courage to forgive his own brother, let alone himself, for that matter. Therefore, reconciliation was out of the question.

"You two can leave now."

Jung's reaction brought about great sorrow upon the pair, and as they began to make their way to the exit through which they en-

EAST FREELAND: ART STORY ONE

tered, Kato imparted one last reflection for the 7 Streeter to ponder.

"You two will need one another, and perhaps one day, you'll see."

As the hour stood still, Jung monitored their departure with a profound sadness, one that exhibited a missed opportunity to honor his father and the realization of a brotherly bond that might be lost forever.

WHISPERING SECRETS

EAST FREELAND: ART STORY ONE

A decorative bell just above the entrance chimed as Eddie and Kenji entered the last shop along their journey with an unmistakable glare of curiosity as they marveled at an assortment of captivating blooms and hues spread neatly before them.

The city's eventful workday had drawn to a close, and as for Whispering Blossoms, the floral mart took on a hushful stillness as the merciful acts of the shop's enchanting assortment's tempting hues welcomed them with delight.

Tracking the Inspector from the door was the onset of the evening, clinging to shelves lined with empty pots behind an aged cash register atop the service counter, and where the airy wisps of botanical fragrances danced in his company with a rhythm of secretive retellings, formed a veil that hung over every object, including Kenji.

Then, with an unmistakable reverence, an indistinct yet humble presence imbued with

WHISPERING SECRETS

a profound appreciation for nature's splendor arose from the rear enclosure of the setting without disturbing the ambiance permeated by the blooms.

"Welcome back, Inspector." The shopkeeper's eyes, always keen even in the dim light, closed in on Eddie. "I trust your journey's end has not disappointed." As if sensing the florist's profound purpose, Kenji gradually settled by the Inspector's feet, ears perked but watchful.

"The pleasure is mine, Mr. Ko…it seems Freeland has even more layers than I can remember," Eddie replied with a rather knowing tone.

Thus, with a mild gesture that seemed to brush away a layer of history, Mr. Ko beckoned Eddie closer.

"I sensed a convergence of events that won over your return, Inspector," the storekeeper divulged as he led the way to the service counter for hot tea. "Please, drink."

EAST FREELAND: ART STORY ONE

"What has happened here?" he asked. But soon after they partook in the simmering pot of soothing immersion, Mr. Ko's charmed expression unexpectedly took a turn, hinting at grave matters beyond the imagination.

"Flowers whisper, you know. Astonishingly, they're our society's clever observers and are fantastic listeners, too," said Mr. Ko. However, there was a dense pause, leaning toward a crucial element that was significant to Eddie's journey. "But it was I who arranged your assignment, Inspector."

"Ahh, I see. You are a Spymaster; and this shop, your apron, and these rare floral specimens are your cover?" Eddie learned.

"Whispering Blossoms has long served the guardians of Freeland City in more ways than one. It's a haven, a safe house for those who, like you, can untangle the dangers that threaten to separate this town."

"But what about Ricky? He's able, aren't he?" questioned the Inspector. But after wit-

WHISPERING SECRETS

nessing the nervy cadet's fighting abilities, backed by Kato and the entire force at Unity East, he appeared unstoppable—so Eddie believed.

"Ah, Ricky," he mentioned. "His longing for admiration blinds him at times, but if you are referring to the incident that ensued here earlier with the 7 Streeters, it was an opportunity to gauge him as a potential ally—a crucible, one might say. And once I witnessed the burning rage behind his fists that fueled his ambitions to stop Jung, I chose not to intervene."

"And what about this convergence you spoke of, what can you share?" Amidst their exchange, a gentle rustle whispered through the shop, reaching the soft pink-shaded petals of a brave blossom tree that chose this silent hour to celebrate its brief phenomenon.

"Her wickedness is unlike any challenge we have faced before," Mr. Ko whispered as if the walls surrounding them could betray them

EAST FREELAND: ART STORY ONE

both. "She is as mysterious as she is cunning. Thus, I urge you to exercise caution, for she has already taken root here in Freeland."

Blossoming like a colorful brushstroke against the somber backdrop of the public establishment, a rousing floral display burst forth, serving as a muted chorus to the pivotal exchange that had taken place between the two operatives.

"Well, it appears my furry companion, and I have much to see and much more to undo here, Mr. Ko." Afterward, Eddie stood to bow before the sage, inviting Kenji to do the same.

"In deed…this way." Leading to another slot within the mart of secrets, Mr. Ko motioned towards a secluded compartment prepared for Eddie's leisure with a meaningful nod. "Rest now, for tomorrow carries great peril, Inspector."

JEALOUSY TAKES HOLD

EAST FREELAND: ART STORY ONE

In the calm corners of the Unity East precinct, stealthy footfalls crept through the halls, weaving a path toward the sacred Unity Martial Arts Center.

Passing through the shadows with silent intent, the intruder drew nearer while the peaceful ambiance, a gift of Freeland's nightly sky, set the stage for a meaningful lesson and maybe more.

Sliding the entry open, the trespasser was stumped to find First Sergeant Kato seated in deep meditation at the core of the training floor.

"Shit."

The lunar glow, seeping in through the main pane, outlined the sharp lines around Kato's eyes, his mighty frame, and the steady rise and fall of his breath as he focused inward, seemingly undisturbed by the intruder's existence as if he had been expecting this moment all along.

"Still sneaking into my precinct like a

JEALOUSY TAKES HOLD

laughable Shinobi, Jung? You could have just knocked," he jeered.

Astonished by Kato's ability to discern an invader's presence, even in the dead of night, Jung advanced warily, stepping inside one bare foot at a time.

"I came to train—to find relief under your protection, old man," he admitted. Even after the toughest of quarrels to ensue between both him and his brother, Jung always returned to the station to practice, winning the respect of a father who longed for his child.

"I, too, seek peace and balance here, just as you two once did. Under my care, watching you, Ricky, and even Jenni develop your talents was like a privilege that I will cherish for an eternity. But, you all have grown apart in many ways, and I must know…do you hate him?" Jung hesitated, believing that the shakedown at his Hate Club was more than an investigation over the contraband and its bizarre origins.

EAST FREELAND: ART STORY ONE

"Ricky's actions tonight were a deliberate attack on my character!" he retorted. "He doesn't even respect me, you know. And who does he think he is, huh? Outing me in front of everyone like that—baiting me with that fucking gun as if I can't control my side of this fucking town, huh? He humiliated me!"

Detecting Jung's fiery emotions rising to the forefront, Kato recognized the profound scars of shame and anguish that had festered inside his son for so very long. He could identify the telltale signs of a young rebel scarred by the community's intolerance towards him, and yet, beneath that seething madness lay a profound sorrow, a well of pain born from years of being excluded and misunderstood. This, Kato knew, or so he believed.

"Your anger is justified, but Ricky swore an oath to protect the citizens of this community. He has proven his merit just as all other cadets have under my watch, and although his actions, however impulsive they

JEALOUSY TAKES HOLD

may seem, stem from a deep-rooted sense of duty instilled within every man and woman attached to this precinct. Perhaps you should honor him just the same, even if his methods differ from your own," he stated, measured and firm.

"You've always favored Ricky over me."

The accusation rattled the entire station as it threatened to suffocate the already tense affair, and despite Kato's open efforts to mend their fraying connection, Jung's unchecked jealousy morphed into a forceful roundhouse kick, striking the emblem of unity that stood as a bystander to their private session.

CRASH!

Fallen into two slivering pieces, the shattered banner, due to Jung's violent outburst, mirrored a sensitive rift that compelled Kato to address the wreckage of their familial fellowship.

"Why desecrate a symbol of our strength and togetherness, Jung? We are a family." Ex-

EAST FREELAND: ART STORY ONE

ploring the torn remnants of unity at his feet, Kato's heart ached as an emotional recollection surfaced—a vision of Ricky and Jung practicing together as equals in the very dojo that now bore witness to their strained brotherhood. "You two were once inseparable… what exactly happened for you to carry such hatred for him?" he asked.

"You're so pretentious that you still fail to accept your hand in all of this, old man," Jung declared, yet, sensing his son's inner turmoil, Kato remained motionless, allowing his stillness to penetrate Jung's very soul.

"I've come to terms with many things that have occurred during my lifetime, and your battles hold no greater weight than those of others," he stated. Jung's throat instantly tightened, narrowing with a wave of guilt. "And unless you pardon yourself and each member of this family, the fury simmering inside your soul will ultimately devour you, my child."

JEALOUSY TAKES HOLD

Kato's words rang true, and despite this realization, Jung's obsession with Ricky being the better brother continued to beset him, a crippling dependence that had taken root and threatened to spiral out of control.

"Unless you address the agony you've caused, there can be no mending of our relationship, you murderer," Jung concluded, and with that grave charge remaining, he disappeared into the moonlit night like a shadow dancer, leaving the Sumo Champion to wrestle with the profound weight and formidable challenges that lay ahead in their wounded, and unresolved past.

As the echoes of Jung's accusation faded into the halls of the agency, Kato's broad shoulders gradually slumped under the weight of unspoken regrets. But, unbeknownst to him, a silent witness, drawn by the commotion, remained as still as the pain that hung over her father; It was Jenni.

"I'm scared, too," she whispered.

EAST FREELAND: ART STORY ONE

Battling the urge to rush to her father's side, she locked the wheels of her chair and watched as Kato began to collect all the pieces of the broken unity symbol. She had never seen him appear to be so defeated, for he had always been a pillar of strength in her life.

From her vantage point, Jenni's mind raced, piecing together fragments of discussions she had heard over the years. She had always known there was tension between Jung and the rest of the family, but the depth of the rift shocked her, raising questions she had never dared to ask.

EAST FREELAND POLICE DEPARTMENT

54th

To: First Sergeant Kato
From: Captain Jenni
Subject: Jung's Behavior and Motivations

Father,

Jung, the leader of the 7 Streeters, embodies a complex mix of authority, anger, and addiction. Marked by a cruel desire for power and control, he rules his criminal empire through fear and intimidation with an iron fist. However, his judgment is often clouded by his reliance on drugs, which he believes enhance his fighting abilities. This addiction exacerbates his violent tendencies and unpredictable nature. Despite this, I believe Jung's motives are driven by a need for belonging and validation, having been rejected by society and even his own brother, Ricky, and although his actions are often brutal, they obviously stem from a place of pain and a misguided quest for respect in a world that once shunned him.

With determination and honor,
Captain Jenni

BECOMING WANTED

BECOMING WANTED

As a performer in this story, I am grateful for the opportunity to contribute to the changing landscape of the entertainment industry. I believe in the transformative power of storytelling, and "East Freeland" represents my commitment to creating narratives that resonate with authenticity and inclusivity.

Becoming Jung, for example, was more than a tricky role to embrace, let alone execute; he challenged me to face my past fears as a mixed American. But on a lighter note, I learned how to use the Nunchaku, and man… was it painful.

In conclusion, "East Freeland" is more than just a tale; it reflects my passion, and I hope it leaves a lasting impact, encouraging others to embrace their unique journeys and the power of representation in all its forms.

Regards,
David

FURIOUS OUTCOMES

FURIOUS OUTCOMES

The Butcher's Passage, an aisle reserved for those who could stomach the fishy odor of the slaughter, seeped a rancid taste of iron affixed to the suspended formations of clanking chains and stained meat hooks exposed by a line of crackling bulbs that marked the path for the port's bald overseer.

Shouldering aside a barrier of red-stained strip curtains, the noise of his toes slogging through the gruesome muck of the pit indicated his arrival as he united with six of his most devoted, becoming the seventh to form a ring around the slick adversary who had confronted Ricky at the Bidder's Den.

They offered no emotion, nor did they exhibit any guilt. Their motorcycle helmets, black as ink, mirrored the traitor's bleeding despair, while their rough leather knuckles dripped with unnecessary roughness, all of which added to the unsettling backdrop of their leader's heartless disposition.

"You were aware of the forbidden pos-

EAST FREELAND: ART STORY ONE

session of a firearm in this town, and yet, in the face of a police officer, you still pulled the trigger," Jung accused.

The silence that followed was punctuated only by the distant hum of the clashing waters outside. And then, without another word, he reached out and removed one of the biker's helmets only to send it crashing into the renegade's face.

WHACK!

"YOU ARE A DISGRACE TO YOUR BROTHERS! HOW COULD YOU LEAD AN ENTIRE CADET FORCE HERE?" His message was as loud as it was clear. It was a warning to all who dared to cross the 7 Streeters, but even worse, to defy him was a death warrant signed and dated. "Where did you get that fucking gun?" he pressed. Yet, as Jung closed in, the bleeding man's ruptured eye twitched with defiance, a moment that shook the others encircling him.

"She's coming to take this town, and

FURIOUS OUTCOMES

when she does, every single citizen, cadet, and 7 Streeter will surrender to her regime." Even in the face of Jung, whom he no longer served, the defector's resolve was still intact and practically unshakable.

"Is that right?" With that, Jung's sudden stillness sent shudders down the ridges of those present until he liberated his Nunchaku from around his neck, following a series of bone-shattering strikes that took the gunman's face apart with untamed fury.

WHAM—WHAM—WACK—WACK!

The crack of the chain-linked weapon against flesh snapped the silence of the entire passage, and with each lash growing faster and faster, every blow was a testament to his relentless will to maintain control and uphold his wicked reign.

WACK—WHAM—WACK—WACK!

Jung's wrath became a living thing fueled by the immorality repressed deep within him. But as for his loyal Streeters, they watched as

EAST FREELAND: ART STORY ONE

their former brother's blood splattered onto their face shields while his savage demise seeped into the fabric of their devotion, for this was the price of disloyalty in the unforgiving nature of their world.

To Be Continued...

www.becomewanted.com

www.ingramcontent.com/pod-product-compliance
Lightning Source LLC
LaVergne TN
LVHW021952060526
838201LV00049B/1673